UNIV
Press

THE **RED CHESTERFIELD**

Wayne Arthurson

Brave & Brilliant Series
ISSN 2371-7238 (Print) ISSN 2371-7246 (Online)

University of Calgary Press
2500 University Drive NW
Calgary, Alberta
Canada T2N 1N4
press.ucalgary.ca

LIBRARY AND ARCHIVES CANADA CATALOGUING IN PUBLICATION

Title: The red chesterfield / Wayne Arthurson.
Names: Arthurson, Wayne, 1962- author.
Series: Brave & brilliant series ; no. 11. 2371-7238
Description: Series statement: Brave & brilliant series, 2371-7238 ; 11
Identifiers: Canadiana (print) 20190103019 | Canadiana (ebook) 20190103035 | ISBN 9781773850771 softcover) | ISBN 9781773850788 (PDF) | ISBN 9781773850795 (EPUB) | ISBN 9781773850801 (Kindle)
Classification: LCC PS8551.R888 R43 2019 | DDC C813/.6—dc23

The University of Calgary Press acknowledges the support of the Government of Alberta through the Alberta Media Fund for our publications. We acknowledge the financial support of the Government of Canada. We acknowledge the financial support of the Canada Council for the Arts for our publishing program.

Printed and bound in Canada by Marquis
♻ This book is printed on Rolland Opaque Natural FSC paper

Editing by Aritha van Herk
Copyediting by Ryan Perks
Cover image: Colourbox 8004416 and 34794621
Cover design, page design, and typesetting by Melina Cusano

To the memory of my father,
George A. Arthurson

The Red Chesterfield

There is a Red Chesterfield in the ditch at the end of the road. Some may call it a sofa or even use the more common American vernacular, a couch. But it is obviously a chesterfield, big enough to seat three, possibly four adults. Too small to be a sofa. And even though it is tossed haphazardly into the ditch, there is a formality to the piece. Maybe it's the Davenport design, but when one looks at it, the word "couch" does not come to mind. Couch denotes an informality, like those ubiquitous black leather couches on which young men play video games, watch sports, and spill their beers and snacks. That is a couch.

The object in the ditch is a chesterfield. Red. Which is what I write in my notebook, noting the location, time, and date.

Red Chesterfield.

The Yard Sale

"Are you connected in any way to that Red Chesterfield?"

"What the fuck are you talking about?" The man turns and sees my uniform and changes his language. "Sorry, I didn't see you there," he says. I notice that despite his apology, the dismissive tone in his voice is still present.

He speaks with an Eastern European accent, and despite my efforts not to do so, I immediately try to place it. Polish? Ukrainian? Belarussian perhaps? But I quickly brush aside those prejudiced thoughts.

"Can I help you?" the man says. The question is followed by a series of deep, hacking coughs and the spitting of some phlegm. Possibly some type of pulmonary obstruction disease. He's turned to face me, hands on his hips to look more threatening. But despite the many threats I've faced for my ticket writing, no one has ever physically assaulted me.

"Do you know anything about the Red Chesterfield?" I ask, pointing down to the end of the road.

He squints in its direction. "Nothing to do with me," he says, coughing and spitting once more. I know he's only pretending to see. I note that and then look around at his yard. Yes. This is the place that was reported. This is where I'm supposed to be now. I put aside the Red Chesterfield.

The Yard Sale (Possibly Illegal)

On a yellow tarp stretched between two upright hockey sticks the words are printed in black magic marker: YARD SALE. But this is not a typical yard sale. The coughing/spitting man's front yard is filled with what can only be termed junk—the details did not register at first because junk is just junk. It has no resemblance to the leftover bits that average people collect in their lives, forget about, outgrow, and then sell in their yard sales. This is something else.

"How long have you held this yard sale?"

"Two days," he quickly says.

"My report says this was running last week. Not really a definition of a yard sale."

"The bylaw says yard sales can't run three consecutive days and I haven't done that. This week was only two days, last week the same."

"You keep the sign up all the time."

"So what. I don't sell stuff then. Only on weekends. So it's a yard sale."

I look over the yard again at tables covered with household appliances and tools, books, faded toys, cutlery, plates, cups, saucers, shoes, boots, boxes filled children's clothes, nuts, bolts, nails, screws, drill bits, washers, hammers, wrenches, and screwdrivers. Hundreds of hockey and lacrosse sticks, baseballs bats, tennis, badminton, squash, and racquetball racquets, laying on both sides of the sidewalks. A line of vacuum cleaners, shovels, rakes, and lawn mowers. One industrial-sized upright freezer, missing a door. And so much more.

After a moment he asks: "You going to give me a ticket?"

After a moment I shake my head. "No. Not today. Just a warning."

He smiles, spitting once more on the ground in front of me.

This Fucking City

As I open the door to my truck, I hear a voice. "You gonna do something about the yard sale?"

I turn to see a middle-aged man approaching me from a house across the street. He wears a bathrobe over his pyjamas, his feet tucked into a pair of slippers.

"I'm investigating the complaint," I tell him.

"Yeah but are you going to do something about it?"

It's city policy not to reveal such information, but like the yard sale bylaw, it's a fluid policy. "I will first issue a warning."

"A warning? That's it. A fucking warning? It's been like that for weeks. It's ruining the neighbourhood."

"That's the protocol, sir."

The man stares at me for several seconds and then shakes his head. "Jesus fuck," he says. "This fucking city."

The Red Chesterfield Redux

Unable to shake my thoughts about the Red Chesterfield, I head out of the cul de sac and approach the ditch from the other side. I park by the side of the road and climb out of my vehicle.

From this point of view, I can now see that it's a bit more damaged on the back than the front, with a couple of good-sized rips in the fabric. For some reason this bothers me, that someone would treat a chesterfield in such a manner.

Something sticks out from one of the holes, a shoe it looks like. I step into the ditch to get a better look.

It's a shoe. A Nike sneaker. White but with many scuffs. Maybe it's because I'm looking for some reason behind the discarding of such a decent piece of furniture, or maybe I don't like how the scuffed sneaker takes away from overall gestalt of this Red Chesterfield—I do have a tendency for order, which is one reason I make a good bylaw officer—but I grab the sneaker.

To my surprise, there's more heft to the sneaker than expected. I pull it out and, to my further surprise, there's a foot cut off at the ankle still in the shoe.

I drop the shoe.

I Have a Headache

I have a headache. It's because of the police lights. I don't know why every police vehicle needs to keep their lights flashing like this. I understand one or two to set up some kind of perimeter. But all of them? It doesn't make sense, which tells me there must be some kind of policy behind the need to keep flashing their lights. Or maybe they just like flashing lights, like little kids at the fairgrounds.

Police swarm around the Red Chesterfield, poking and prodding, looking at the ground in the ditch, the road on my side and on the cul de sac, searching for clues. I'm pretty sure the constant flashing of blue and red lights isn't helping them find any clues. Especially as the sun is starting to set.

A small crowd of people, including the neighbour in slippers, have gathered on the cul de sac side, watching the excitement. The yard sale proprietor with the pulmonary obstruction disease had been there, but he left, making a call on his phone as he walked back to his house.

For me, there is nothing to do but wait. Even though I made a preliminary statement to the first responders I know I'll have to make a more detailed one. I listen to a radio program; someone is being interviewed about a book about the importance of clutter and keeping old things, but the interviewer isn't listening to what's being said, only going from prepared question to prepared question.

My headache intensifies, so I shut my eyes to the lights. It helps but I can still see the flashing through my eyelids.

Fingerprints

I jump at the sound of someone tapping on my window. I catch my breath and touch the button to lower the glass.

A plainclothes police officer greets me with a smile. I chastise myself internally for being surprised at her gender. I should know better.

"You found the foot?" she asks.

I nod. Then I fill her in on the circumstances, trying to be as concise as possible. She takes detailed notes.

"So you touched the shoe?" she asks when I finish.

"I'm sorry."

"Am I right to assume that due to your position with the city, you have no criminal record?"

"You are right to assume that."

She takes a deep breath. "We'll need to get your fingerprints."

Fingerprints Part 2

An hour later. The lights still flash but the crowd of bystanders has dissipated. Pyjama Man remains with a couple of onlookers. Mr. Yard Sale showed up once again, still talking on his phone, but then left again. The interviewer on the radio is talking to a panel of people about the Oilers' lack of secondary scoring and the need for a right-hand defenceman on the power play. The panelists pretend to disagree even though they agree with this assessment. I'm kept awake by my annoyance of this discussion.

A uniformed constable taps on my window. He sports a goatee to look older, but it doesn't suit his face. Or his uniform.

"You're supposed to come with me," he says.

"Do you mean go with you? Or do I follow you in my vehicle?"

"That wasn't specified, but probably best if you come with me so you don't get lost."

"Where are we going?"

"West District."

"I know where that is. I can drive myself."

"I'm not sure about that. Best if you leave your vehicle here. I can drive you back."

"Please, I live nearby there. It would be much easier if I drove myself."

The uniformed officer walks away, saying nothing. I watch him talk to the plainclothes detective. She turns to look at me sitting in my truck. After a moment, she nods.

"Okay, follow me," the constable says when he returns.

Lost

The constable takes a right when he should have taken a left. I debate whether to follow him. I don't. I arrive at the West District on my own.

I enter the doors and after a moment the receiving constable waves me forward. He's older and chubby, probably a couple of years from retirement, hasn't chased down a suspect in years. He asks why I'm there and I tell him. He chuckles behind his bulletproof glass. "Have a seat. Someone will be with you in a minute."

I sit, pick up a magazine about gardening, put it down. I don't want to read about compost; I just want to go home.

Lost No Longer

I hear laughter in the background. It's coming from inside the station, drifting through the bulletproof glass.

A second later there's a buzz, and the lost, goateed constable comes through a door from the back and enters the reception area. He is blushing and there's an embarrassed yet angry look on his face. I stand up slowly, waving to get his attention but then realize that this is a mistake. The embarrassment flees his face, leaving only anger. I quickly lower my hand.

"Please come with me," he snaps. The blush rises again.

I don't make eye contact as I come up to the door. I'm pretty sure his colleagues are punishing him by making us wait for almost five seconds before they buzz us in. He opens the door with one hand and, with the other on my shoulder, pushes me through the door.

I stumble but catch myself. I could complain because I'm not a criminal, I'm only a witness. But I know better. I just step aside as he closes the door behind us.

"Please keep up," he says. "I don't want you to—" He stops himself from saying the words "get lost." Blushes again.

I follow him, into the main part of the West District station, into the laughter of his fellow colleagues.

Fingerprints Part 3

The constable seems sorry for pushing me through the door. He doesn't look at me when he takes my fingerprints, he just focuses on the task, saying nothing. His touch is also very delicate, like I'm a piece of porcelain he doesn't want to break.

He takes my fingerprints gently, rolling my thumb and each finger onto the ink pad and then onto the paper with simple professionalism.

When he's done and I'm wiping the ink off my fingers with the provided towel, I thank him.

He blushes again. "I'm sorry I handled you roughly before. And the door. If you wish to file a complaint, I won't contest it."

"That's okay. I understand."

"You shouldn't have to understand. I was wrong in how I handled you. You should file a complaint."

"I'm not going to file a complaint."

He looks at me and then, after a moment, nods. "Thanks." He gestures with his hand, showing me the way forward. "Let me show you the way out."

Once he realizes what he says, he laughs. I join in.

Pull Over

I'm still chuckling as I walk across the parking lot to my vehicle.

But once I'm driving down the road away from the police station, I'm reminded why I was there. I see the Red Chesterfield in the ditch. I see it from the front, where it looks untouched and harmless. And then I see it from the back, where it is torn, with a shoe that still had a foot cut off at the ankle inside. I only saw the foot for a brief second before I dropped it, but I remember every detail. The bone of the foot, the tendons and muscles around it, exposed to the air, the tangle of skin hanging off the spot where the ankle ends, lines of dried blood, the wriggling of maggots digging their way under the skin, a couple of them dropping onto my hand.

I pull over.

It's a long time before I can start driving again.

Late

It's completely dark by the time I get home. I open the front door to the bungalow, my face clear of tears and anguish. All the lights are on; not unexpected, since everyone should be home.

I don't shout out a greeting because no one will shout back. I put my jacket in the closet and hang my keys on the hook. There is a stack of mail in the basket by the door but none of it is for me.

I turn left down the hallway and then right into the bathroom, where I disrobe, dropping my clothes down the chute into the basement laundry room.

It takes several seconds for the hot water to come up the pipes, and several more for me to adjust the temperature. I step in and wash the day from my body.

It takes longer than usual because of the foot found in the shoe found in the Red Chesterfield.

After my shower, I go to my room and get dressed in a pair of sweat pants and a T-shirt. Then into the kitchen to heat up some leftovers, a meatloaf and some rice I made a couple days ago.

With my bowl and spoon in hand, I go to talk to my brother.

The Older Brother

My older brother K sits at the dining room table, a mess of papers in front of him. He has what looks to be a booklet with a list of names and addresses in it next to a small Chromebook I haven't seen before. He types on the Chromebook, looking at the name and addresses, which gives me the impression he is entering these names and addresses.

I sit across from him and eat my meal, watching him for several minutes.

"How was your day?" he asks, without looking up.

"Interesting." I contemplate telling him about the Red Chesterfield and the foot.

But when he says, "That's nice," with a casual indifference, I know he is only being polite. He will not be interested. He is deeply focused on his form creation and I've known my brother long enough to know that if he is focused on something, there is no point trying to distract him. He is more stubbornly attentive than I am.

But I do ask him one question. "Where is J?"

Again, my brother responds without looking up, without stopping his work. "Where do think?"

Flashback

My older brother and I decided to go to the movies. To the new theatre thirteen blocks to the east because it had many theatres instead of only one, plush seats, and sound that seemed to vibrate the building. It was glorious.

As we came out of the matinee, our senses overloaded, I saw that there was a Sylvester Stallone movie playing in another theatre. "I love Stallone," I said.

"Come with me," my brother said, grabbing my arm and pulling me into the bathroom.

"Give me your jacket," he said, once we were in.

I did. He put it on, handing me his.

"Wrap it around your waist, like it's too hot and you don't want to carry it anymore."

I did that.

He turned us toward the mirror and looked us over. After a second, he nodded. "Perfect. Let's go."

"Where are we going?"

"Just follow me. Act natural, but don't say anything."

I followed him into the theatre that was about to show the Stallone movie. I acted natural. I said nothing.

It was glorious.

Unhealthy Routines

I fear K is doing what we did in that theatre: creating fake identities out of existing ones. I'd like to talk to him about it, to challenge him, but at the moment the stress of my day tells me to ignore it.

J

Anyway, I have to go down to the basement to do my laundry. There, in the small living space that was built into the basement by a previous owner of the house, sits my younger brother J. He is slouched on his black leather couch in front of his TV playing a violent first-person shooter game. His couch is a true couch, the total opposite of the Red Chesterfield in the ditch.

I watch him from behind, watch him destroy aliens for a little bit, but I can't help but look at the back of the couch, reminded of the find in the Red Chesterfield. I move to the side of the couch to escape that vision. But also so he can see I am there. I don't want him to think I am spying on him.

"Hey M," J says when he sees me in his peripheral vision. But he does not look at me directly. To do so could cause his avatar to get killed. I have played these games as well and know what kind of concentration it takes to succeed.

"How was school?"

"The same, you know. School's school." He kills a couple more aliens to get to a checkpoint. "How was work?"

Again, I feel a small compulsion to tell J my story. I know it would interest him enough to make him stop his game and pay attention to me. But he would have so many questions about the foot that I would have to take another shower to get back to normal again. And I don't want to stress him out.

"The same, you know. Work's work."

Flashback #2

"What should we tell him?" my older brother asked.

"The truth?" I replied.

"We can't do that. He won't be able to handle it. He'll cry all the time."

"He'll cry anyway. You can't stop him."

"But I can't tell him the truth. It's a stupid way for them to die. I'm going to say they were killed in a car accident."

"He'll find out. Maybe not now because he's young, but when he's older, he'll find out."

"I'll cross that when I come to it."

"I think you should tell him the truth. Lying about it will just make breaking the news harder."

"No. This is for the best.

"I disagree."

"You'll never understand. Never."

"Understand what?"

"Why I have to make these decisions. It's my job."

"Your job?

"To protect you. Both of you. Especially with Momma and Da now gone."

Laundry

I throw my uniform into the washer along with some coloured clothes that the others have thrown down. I see a maggot wriggle out of a sleeve. I jump back, slamming the door. I shake my arm to get rid of any phantom remnants. The laundry gets a full cap of detergent and the hottest temperature possible.

On my way back upstairs, I ask J if he will transfer them to the dryer before he goes to bed.

"Sure, no problem."

And I know he will, because that's kind of person he is. K would not do the same. But he has other attributes.

With that taken care of, I go into my room and lie on my bed, starting to read a book about a forgotten inventor. I only last a couple of pages before I feel my head start to droop. I close the book, saving my page with my bookmark, shut off my light, and lie flat.

I nevertheless find it difficult to fall asleep in the dark. All I see is the colour red.

And one single maggot coming out of my sleeve.

The Next Day

As soon as I walk through the door, I'm besieged by my co-workers. All of them clamour to know what happened, what the foot looked like, how I'm feeling, whether I need any help, and all those predictable comments and requests. I'm a deer in the headlights, as they say.

But my supervisor, Rhonda, is pushing through the crowd. Rhonda is a small woman but she has a hobby called cross-training, so she's strong and fit.

"Leave M alone," she barks. "Have some respect for a colleague."

There's a moan of disappointment, but the crowd dissipates, reluctantly. Rhonda stands there for a moment, throwing dirty looks to get people on their way, either back to their desks or out the door for their shifts. "Come on, you all have work to do, so get to it."

Once everyone has moved on, Rhonda turns to me, placing a hand on my wrist. Her face softens. "Are you okay?" she asks.

"I'm fine," I say with a nod. "A little flustered by the attention, but I understand why. They are only curious, like I would be."

Rhonda nods encouragingly. But then the touch on my arm becomes a strong grip. She pulls me toward her office, the softness gone from her face.

My Boss Is Also My Girlfriend

Rhonda closes the door behind her, not quite a slam but just about. She releases me from her grip, almost throwing my arm aside. She storms to her side of the desk but doesn't sit down on her chair.

"I tried calling you last night," she snaps. "As soon as I heard, I called."

"I turned my phone off."

"More than ten times I called. I was worried."

"I'm sorry. I just didn't feel like talking."

"Not even to me?"

I sigh. What can I say that won't disappoint my girlfriend? Sure, she is my boss but she was my girlfriend before she was my boss. I mean in the chronological sense; we were dating before she got her promotion. Everyone knew, but no one really cared.

"I'm sorry, Rhonda, yesterday was difficult for me. I found someone's foot in a discarded Red Chesterfield and inadvertently set off a murder investigation. I had to give my fingerprints and DNA to the police so they won't confuse me with the murderer. I just wanted to go home and calm down and forget the day."

The anger in her face fades. She steps around her desk and wraps her arms around me. "I'm so sorry," she says with a sob. "You're right. I'm being selfish." Her sobs become so intense that she can no longer talk.

My shirt front, the one I washed last night, is wet.

Drying Her Eyes

Rhonda looks up at me, her face stained with tears. "You okay?" she asks.

"I've been better, but I'll survive."

"Your poor thing," she says, squeezing me in a hug, one that lasts several seconds. My body sighs with relief in her arms. I wish to stay there. But we can't. We are at work.

She pulls away and walks around to her side of the desk, drying her eyes with her sleeve. She pulls down on her shirt to smooth out the wrinkles in her uniform. "As your boss, I have to officially ask if you are okay."

"And officially, I will reply that I've been better, but I will survive."

She smiles a smile that fills her entire face and reminds me of why I became romantically involved with this co-worker. "At least you still have a sense of humour."

I shrug.

After a moment, she continues. "There is also a list of counsellors for you to choose from if you wish to talk about your experience."

I shake my head.

Rhonda sighs, disappointed at my reticence. But she doesn't push it. She knows me well.

"You can also take time off. It's your decision. But officially, and unofficially, I highly recommend that you go home."

"If I go home, all I'll do is think about what happened yesterday, and—" I pause, banishing the image of the Red Chesterfield and the foot from my mind. "That will only make it worse." Deep breath. "I need to work."

Rhonda nods and writes in a notebook.

"You need another hug?" she asks.

Of course I do.

The New Red Chesterfield

I go about my work. The easy stuff, always the weeds. There is a list of what is a noxious weed and what is not. Unfortunately, not everyone reads that list and thinks any plant other than a perfect lawn is a weed. So, there are a lot of complaints to get through. If the weeds in question aren't noxious, I move on. If they are, I tuck a notice in the mailbox about noxious weeds. This notice is usually all it takes; when I return to check, the weeds are gone. If not, I leave a warning. Ninety-nine point nine per cent of complaints are dealt with after a warning.

The harder complaints are those concerning community standards. These deal with states of houses, if their conditions are detrimental to the neighbourhood. Guidelines can be vague about peeling paint, discarded furniture in back yards, open compost bins, damaged fencing—the list goes on.

Again, notices are left, followed by warnings if nothing happens. This is my day, day in and day out, driving around doing my best to keep the city up to a reasonable standard while not being a hard-ass about what that means.

The time passes well, without my giving much thought to the previous situation. But near the end of the day, I'm in the general vicinity of where I saw the Red Chesterfield and found the foot.

Although I know it's a mistake, I decide to drive past, even though it's not on my way.

As soon as I turn the corner onto the street, I see it. Plain as day, as obvious as the last time.

The Red Chesterfield.

Road Rage

I brake so hard and fast that the driver behind me almost collides with my vehicle. A long blare on his horn as I stare at the item of furniture that I thought the police would have taken away as a key piece of evidence. Why would they leave it behind? More horn blaring when I don't move. He pulls into the oncoming lane, but stops right next to me. I turn and look at him blankly. His window is rolled down and he screams a stream of obscenities at me. I don't hear the words, just the anger. But even that is not enough to move me. I turn away from his shouting and look at the Red Chesterfield.

Is it the same piece of furniture? Or a different one? It looks exactly like the one from yesterday, even with the rips in the back. But surely the police would not have left it behind. It must be another one. Or would they leave it behind? Could they not find a way to transport it? It must be another one.

If so, will there be another foot tucked inside the back?

More importantly, who put it here? Not just this Red Chesterfield, but the other one as well.

Into the Ditch

I know I should call the police, call the detective who took my statement the other night. Even contacting the young constable who got lost on his way to the police station would be a better idea than my pulling my vehicle to the side of the road, getting out, and climbing into the ditch.

But I must see if this Red Chesterfield is real. I must make sure that this is not some post-traumatic hallucination.

Down into the ditch I go, up to the Red Chesterfield. I reach out to touch it, but then pull my hand back. I don't want to make the same mistake again.

For a moment I stare at the Red Chesterfield, look at its Davenport outline, conjecture that if this is not the original, it is an exact copy. A second later, I decide there is only one way to determine if this Red Chesterfield is real and not a hallucination.

I sit.

Heebie-Jeebies

When I sit, I don't fall to the ground. The Red Chesterfield is real.

It is also extremely comfortable, further supporting my belief that this is a chesterfield and not a sofa or a couch. Only chesterfields have this kind of bearing. The springs are well maintained, the fabric soft to the touch without being rubbery. My hands have tactile sensitivity, making them defensively reactive to materials. Velvet and velour give me the heebie-jeebies, while some leathers can be too smooth.

The fabric covering the Red Chesterfield is just the perfect material for my hands, as if designed for me. That thought sends a shiver through my soles. I immediately dismiss that idea as folly. I can be single-minded at times but never to the point of narcissism.

How could anyone have known that I called in the original complaint? And how would they know I would pass the scene again? Whatever is at play cannot be aimed at me. I am just a random link, a player because I found the Red Chesterfield.

The foot.

A random player.

I relax into the Red Chesterfield and think about what I should do.

The Yard Sale Part 2

As I sit on Red Chesterfield #2 my mind turns over thoughts of what to do next. Call the police? Call Rhonda? Look under the cushion? Or just sit and enjoy the comforts of this high-quality piece of furniture. Sitting is the most comfortable option. But while my attention drifts, so does my vision. And on that cul de sac, the most prominent piece of visual stimulus is the yard sale.

The sign is still up, the tarp flapping in the wind whenever a sharp gust blows through. The tables full of junk are still full of junk. In fact, it looks like there is even more junk in the yard, like that spitting man made a run during the night to load up more and place it in his yard.

Some lighter bits have blown off, books and plastic plates, bits of children's clothing, landing on the yard next door, the sidewalk out front, and even the street.

Seeing that debris galvanizes me into action. I have only been able to give a warning because the yard sale was confined to the yard. But now it is causing a public hazard. I rise from the chesterfield and hitch up my belt.

A Ticket

I make my way up the sidewalk, through the tables of junk and old appliances. I write up the ticket as I move, noting the infraction and the fine as I climb the steps to knock on the door. City policy states that employees approaching private homes are to ring the doorbell. There is no doorbell for this house, only two disconnected wires hanging from a small opening at the side of the door. I must knock.

There's no answer to my first knock, nor my second. I switch from knocking to banging my fist.

Inside the house, I hear angry words in another language, the tones suggesting something derogatory.

The door is flung open and the large Eastern European man with the pulmonary obstruction disease stands angrily at the door. "What the fuck do you want?" he shouts. His fists are clenched, as if ready for violence. But his tone calms when he sees it's me.

"You," he says, his face softening. After a pause. "Are you okay?"

I am confused by his question.

"That must have been difficult. Terrible."

I am unable to speak because my plan to be a tough bylaw officer is thrown by his kindness.

"You want to come in for some tea? You could talk about your ordeal. Or not. Although sometimes it's best to talk. Even to a stranger."

When I blink, continue to stand silent, he reaches out, gently pulls on my shoulder. "Come," he says. "Have some tea."

The Bookshelves

He ushers me into his house, gesturing for me to sit on a sofa in his living room while he makes the tea.

I cannot help but be surprised by his abode. Unlike the front yard, his house is tasteful, tidy. The furniture is a mix of modern and classic, and the overall gestalt works. His walls display a mix of artwork and family photos. A TV hangs on the wall across from the sofa, not too big but not too small. It does not dominate the room like some TVs do.

What does dominate the room are the two large bookshelves on either side of the couch. The only untidy spaces in the room, they overflow with books—paperbacks, trade and mass market, hardcovers, large print, coffee-table style, board books for kids, all jammed haphazardly onto the shelves. The subject matter is the same, a jumble of styles, seemingly un-curated.

"Ah, you have found my weakness," my host says in a voice that reminds me of a supervillain. "These are only my favourites. You should see my other rooms, they are filled with books. I can't help but buy books, much to the chagrin of my wife."

Again, I am surprised by this. He has a wife and he loves books.

"Sit, sit," he says, gesturing toward the couch with his chin. He is holding a silver tray. "Have some tea. It will help because you, my friend, look like you need some help."

Tea for Two

He hands me a delicate cup filled with tea, a tiny spoon of jam sitting on the saucer next to the cup. I look at the spoon, not sure what to do with it. Do I eat it? Spread the jam on the cookies sitting on a plate near the teapot?

"Ah, yes, it's family tradition," he says. He holds up his spoon for a second, places it in the tea, stirring. He holds up the empty spoon, raising his eyebrows. "It can be a bit sweet for some but sweets are another weakness of mine." He smiles and sips.

It is a bit sweet for me, but oddly soothing. I take another sip and lean back on the sofa with my saucer. It's a comfortable sofa with a well-used support, much like J's couch in the basement.

"You like books?" my host asks.

"I do, although my tastes are more limited than yours. I read a lot of science fiction."

He leans forward, intrigued by this. "Space opera? Cyberpunk? Post-apocalyptic?"

"A bit across all types. Even crime fiction."

"Yes, that is good," he says, waving a finger. "Don't limit yourself, I always say."

He mentions the name of a writer, an English writer I'm familiar with who has recently passed away. And then off we go, into a discussion of his works, and similar works, and whether a certain series of books translated well in the recent television adaptation. It's a pleasant conversation that has nothing to do with my work or the events of the other day. I have more tea and I find myself relaxing even more into his sofa. Soon, my side of the conversation starts to decline.

He doesn't seem to notice.

I fall asleep.

Dream

I dream . . . of nothing.

Voices

I hear voices. Soft voices, first male, in another language, then female, laughing quietly. After a moment, I hear footsteps move away. I am lying on the sofa, a knitted blanket draped over me. It is still light out, but the angle of the sun has changed.

I prop myself on one elbow. The teacups and tray are put away. A small woman sits on the chair across from me. She reads a paperback.

"You're awake," she says. Her voice is not accented like Yard Sale Man.

"I am," I say, swinging my feet forward to sit up. "I am sorry for that."

"It happens. Yuri said you were tired."

Yuri. Yard Sale Man is named Yuri.

"I was. Tired."

"You discovered the foot. I saw you yesterday in your truck."

I nod.

"I'm sorry. But I'm glad Yuri was here for you. He's got a rough exterior, but he's a marshmallow."

I nod.

After a moment, while she continues to read, I say, "I should go."

"Yuri had to go to work but said you are welcome into our home anytime."

"Thank you. Although that sentiment may change."

"The yard sale," she says, her voice putting quotation marks around the word *yard*.

"I'm sorry."

"Don't be. You have to do your job."

"Yes."

But instead of handing her an infraction ticket with a fine, the one I had written earlier, I issue a written warning to clean up the yard.

She takes it with a smile. "Come back, anytime."

Weeds

"You were in there a long time."

I turn toward the sound of the voice and see it is the neighbour from before, the one with the pyjamas underneath his bathrobe. He stands at the end of his walk, wearing a hoodie and a pair of shorts. And his slippers.

"I hope you gave them what for about this mess."

I walk over so I don't have to shout at him.

"Excuse me?"

"I said I hope you gave them what for about their mess. It's ruining the neighbourhood."

I nod but say nothing about the written warning instead of the ticket. He takes my silence as a positive development.

"Good. About time the fucking city did something about that. I've been complaining for a couple of weeks now."

"We get hundreds of complaints a day and we investigate all of them. I arrived yesterday and gave them a warning. Then I returned today."

"Still took your fucking time."

I look at the neighbour and then at his lawn. I point with my finger. He turns.

"What?"

"Canada Thistle."

"So fucking what?"

"It's a noxious weed. Better remove it."

As I walk away, he shouts at me. "Fuck you."

Chastisement

I storm back to my truck and drive away, my tires spraying gravel. I grumble at the neighbour's rudeness, about the entitlement some people think they have, about the bylaws. But deep down, I am disappointed in myself. I broke a number of rules governing the professionalism of a bylaw enforcement officer.

I entered a citizen's home when I should not have.

While in that home, I accepted an offering of some type, a small one perhaps, but still an offering. Even though I gave them a written warning, my drinking the tea could be construed as a bribe.

I also fell asleep while on duty.

Worst of all, I fell asleep on duty while in a citizen's home after accepting an offering of some type. Many punishments are available for these infractions, including dismissal.

Rhonda would be very disappointed.

I chastise myself as I drive home, my shift officially over even though I spent two hours of it sleeping on Yuri's couch.

It is only when I pull up in front of my house that I realize something.

When I passed the ditch, the Red Chesterfield was gone.

Photo Radar

I jerk my vehicle in gear and peel away from the front of my house, my tires screeching, the smoke of burnt rubber blowing behind me. I race through the city, dodging in and out of traffic, breaking the speed limit. A couple of times, the flash of photo radar follows me. I will be disciplined for these infractions, but I don't care. I need to see for myself that the Red Chesterfield is gone.

I must know if I was just too distracted by the events of the afternoon—my falling asleep on Yuri's couch, dealing with the angry neighbour—to see the couch, even though it was there. Or is the Red Chesterfield, or rather the second Red Chesterfield, gone? And if so, where did it go?

I turn onto the road that the ditch runs alongside. But I'm going in the other direction, so I make a U-turn, so fast that the edge of the vehicle skids away. I fight the truck, turning the steering wheel in the other direction, but the vehicle overcompensates and skids back the other way, onto the road.

A car coming toward me swerves to avoid my flailing back end, its horn blaring. Another turns the other way, but I panic and forget to take my foot off the gas. The back tires screech on the pavement, the rear end goes the other way again, and my vehicle roars forward.

The momentum sends me sideways. My back tires bite into the grass and the truck lifts up on one end and, ever so slowly, tips onto its side.

The Blue Zone

The panic attack that occurs immediately after the accident passes relatively quickly. My heart and breathing rates slow and I'm hanging from my seatbelt, my feet drifting towards the passenger door.

My shoulder hurts. Or my neck? Some type of soft-tissue injury that could have long-term consequences. Part of my brain suggests that I move, but I can't. I just shut down, overwhelmed. The Blue Zone.

I can hear someone pounding on the outside of the window, shouting at me.

"Are you okay?" Over and over.

But the conscious part of my brain doesn't register. It's very difficult for me to react to outward stimuli when I'm in the Blue Zone.

I hear grunting. My door opens. It closes again.

"Fuck," someone shouts. "Give me a fucking hand, will you—shock's starting to set in."

The door opens, stays open, voices grunt in effort, hands reach in and grab me, almost drop me when my seatbelt is undone. But over several moments, and with a lot of effort, I am dragged out of my vehicle and deposited on the grass near the shoulder of the world.

Faces stare at me. I stare back but am unable to make a human connection.

"Jesus, no response at all."

"Yeah, but 911's on its way." Sirens in the distance.

"The dog," I hear myself say. "Did you see the dog?"

"What dog?" an excited voice asks. "Is there a dog in your truck?"

"There was a dog on the road. Did I hit it?"

Maybe a Dog

"There was something about trying to miss a dog."

"Did you see a dog?"

"Nope, only swerving all over the road."

"So, no dog?"

"We only saw the truck swerving before we had to get out of the way. So maybe a dog or something ran in front before we got a chance to see it."

"Did you see a dog or any other animal after the accident, sniffing around, running around or anything?"

"Nope. But maybe it got scared, or it got hit and it's hiding over there?"

"Where?"

"You know, in the ditch back there. Underneath that couch."

"What couch?"

Flashlight

I jump to my feet and start to run.

"Hey," someone shouts.

I don't run far. Just about twenty metres from my upturned vehicle into the ditch where the Red Chesterfield sits.

Unlike this afternoon, the Red Chesterfield is upside down, its stubby wooden legs pointing to the sky.

"It's here! It's here." I point at the piece of furniture, jumping up and down like a little kid.

The constable catches up to me, breathing a bit heavily for such a short run. He places his hand on my shoulder. "What? Is the dog there? Do you see it?"

"You see it too? You see the Red Chesterfield?"

"Yeah, I see it. Is the dog underneath?"

"You see it! You see it!" My mind is full of joy and relief. I was not imagining it; the Red Chesterfield was returned. It had been moved, yes, but it is here now.

"Did you find the dog?" another constable asks.

"I don't know, I'm gonna look," says his partner. He steps forward, flicking on a flashlight. The light shows the red of the chesterfield as he walks around it, bending down to look under.

"Yep there's something under there," he says to his partner. Then to me, "Give me a hand, will ya?"

He sticks one end of the flashlight in his mouth and grabs the chesterfield. I grab the same end and push it up, the other end on the ground. I hold it there as he shines his light on what's underneath.

"Holy fuck," he says. A moment later I see what he sees and drop the Red Chesterfield on him.

Pyjamas

"So, you knew him?" I'm questioned again by the female homicide detective. This time in a room downtown.

"The dead man in the pyjamas? Not personally, no. I met him, in the course of my duties. It was the day I found the foot." Pause. "And today."

"Today? Alive?" Her eyebrows rise.

"I had filed a warning against one of his neighbours and then noticed his noxious weeds. Canada Thistle. I suggested he remove them."

"Did he? Remove the noxious weeds?"

"I don't know. I was going to come back later to check."

"Do you do a lot of bylaw enforcement checks at night?"

"What?"

"I mean, let's just cut to the chase, okay? A red chesterfield is found in a ditch with a severed foot in it. The next day, another red chesterfield is found in the same ditch, this time with a body underneath it?"

I nod quickly. "It's incredible, isn't it?"

"Actually, the most incredible part is that the same person discovered each of the red chesterfields." She gives me a look.

I deflate in my chair. "I know. It's . . ." I search my mind to find the word to describe the situation, how it is affecting me and making me feel.

"*Suspicious.* That's the word you're looking for," says the detective. "I'd also add an adverb. Like *highly.*"

Candour

I come clean. I don't worry about the professional repercussions because being fired is always more favourable than being tried for murder. Or any other crime. I tell the detective everything, from the time I first discovered the Red Chesterfield, to the finding of the foot, to having tea and falling asleep in Yuri's house, then racing back and causing the accident.

To give her credit, she does not interrupt me, even though she has heard some of this story from the other day. She takes notes, nods, and lets me ramble. Which I do. A lot.

When I think I'm finished, she says nothing. Just waits. And I add another ten minutes of rambling to fill that silence. This happens once more when I add an apology for not including information that I forgot to mention at the beginning.

She smiles. "Thank you for your candour, this was extremely enlightening." Closes her notebook, pen in pocket. Stands up, adjusts her jacket. "We're going to ask you to wait here for several moments. Someone will bring you a sandwich and a drink. Any requests?"

"Any sandwich will do."

"Drink?"

"Anything—no wait. No cream soda. I hate cream soda."

"Done. And thank you again." She turns to head out of the room.

"Detective?"

She turns back.

"The constable . . . um, the one I . . ."

"Dropped the chesterfield on?" she asks with a smile.

I nod.

"He's fine. Pissed at you, which is why he won't be involved in this case, but overall he's fine."

Worries

I wait and wait and wait, and wonder what is being said about me, who is doing the talking, and what they will decide.

I wonder if they will handcuff me and charge me with murder, lock me up in the Remand Centre until a trial. I wonder how a charge like that would affect my family. Will it dash my older brother's political hopes?

Will J's marks be affected?

And Rhonda? No doubt she will end our relationship, but will this affect her position, especially since she was just promoted?

So many worries.

Especially the cost.

We cannot afford the legal fees.

Release

"You can go."

I snap awake to find myself resting my head on the table. A puddle of drool. I look up. "You," I say.

The constable from the other night, the one who got lost trying to lead me to the West Division station, is standing by an open door.

"Yes. Me." He smiles. "You can go."

I sit up. "I'm not charged with murder or anything like that?"

Shake of the head.

"Wow. That's fantastic." It takes me a minute to process that information. And yes, it's a whole minute—sixty seconds—not just a vague description of time. Finally, I stand up, wiping the drool from my face.

I sign some papers, without reading them but happily, because these papers will allow me to leave the building.

The constable leads me through a maze of hallways but he does not get lost here. We reach an outside door and he opens it, standing aside to let me pass.

"You can go. But I must tell you that technically you are a suspect."

"A suspect."

He nods. Then smiles.

"But not a serious one. More of a person of interest. Someone will be in touch with you later on, but I wouldn't worry about it."

I nod a thanks and step to the door. When I am halfway through he lays a hand on my shoulder, stopping me.

"Don't leave town." Hand lifts.

Greetings

Rhonda shouts my name and rushes to greet me. She pulls me into her embrace and I accept it fully, wrapping my arms around her. Tears flow, especially mine.

It's hard to describe the joy I'm feeling. A few minutes ago, I was held against my will. Legally of course, but no one wishes to be held in custody by authorities, no matter how respectable and friendly those authorities may be. My people have a long history with the authorities, a lot of it bad. And now, I am not only free to go but Rhonda is here, wrapping her arms around me. She takes all the negative energy that has been in me for the last couple of days and sucks it out of me. But she doesn't take it on herself, she just takes it away from me and lets it drift and fade away, like smoke in the wind.

"Rhonda," I whisper.

She grabs my head in her hands and kisses me, deeply, tongues entwined. She's my lover, so this is how we kiss when we are so glad to see each other.

After a moment, another long embrace.

Then a hand on my shoulder. We pull away.

J is standing next to us, smiling. Glad to see me. "Glad you're out."

"J."

I hug him, not as deeply as Rhonda because he's my brother. But it's a strong hug. We have that relationship.

"Where is—" I look about.

J shrugs. "In the car. You know what he's like."

I do.

Backseat

I make a move to get into the front seat, the shotgun seat. "Get in the back," my older brother says.

"Don't be a dick, man," J says to him, standing behind me. Rhonda says nothing but climbs into the seat behind my older brother, quietly making her point.

"In. The. Back." he says, his voice firm.

J pushes me and opens the back door so he can climb in. "Let's just go, okay."

"In the back!" he says to me. "I will not allow you to sit next to me."

"Jesus, sometimes you are a huge dick, man," shouts J.

"I am not the one who was arrested by the police."

"There was no arrest; M was just taken in for questioning."

"Semantics will not change the fact of M's actions. So M will sit in the back."

"You're one to talk."

I let my brothers argue as if I am not even there. Eye contact with Rhonda. She nods and climbs out of the van. I walk around J and join her. We walk away as she touches her phone.

"Hey, where are you going?" J asks.

"Uber" is all I say.

A pause. "Now look what you've done, you dickhead." Car door slams. "Drive home by yourself."

A Ride Home

"Hey guys," J shouts. "Wait up."

Rhonda and I turn and wait for him.

"Jesus, what a dickhead, eh?" J says when he catches up to us.

"He's just looking out for the family," Rhonda says.

"He's just looking out for himself. As per usual."

"K is K," I say. "He can't really help who he is, sometimes. Best to ignore him and move on."

"But he's being a dick."

"And we really can't change that. The only thing we can affect is our reaction. I choose to walk away."

"And let him push you around. Like you always do."

I stop and look at J. "If you wish to come with us in the Uber, then you'll have to stop talking like this."

"But . . . you always—"

I raise my hand to stop him. "I really don't need a lecture today, J. From you or from K. All I need is a ride home."

The van pulls up in front of us. All the doors open automatically.

"Get in," he says. After a moment: "Please."

Without a word, I climb into the front seat, Rhonda gets into the back.

"You coming?" I say to J.

"What about the Uber?" J asks.

Rhonda puts on her seatbelt. "What Uber?"

Spoon

J leans forward to say something to K but Rhonda places her hand on his shoulder. She shakes her head. He looks at her for a second, then sits back, looking out the window. In the side-view mirror I can see his face, scowling.

For the rest of the ride home, nobody says anything. We pull up to the house and even before K puts the van in gear, J is out the vehicle, storming toward the house. He roughly unlocks the door and stomps in, no doubt heading to his basement.

K gets out wordlessly, but much slower, his body stiffened into a passive aggressive posture. I wait several seconds until I know both my brothers are in the house and into their respective rooms. Only then do Rhonda and I get out.

She smiles gently at me and takes my hand, leads into the house. She doesn't let go when we walk in but guides me to my room. Only then does she release my hand, turning me around to face her. A light kiss on the cheek. She removes my shirt, gently pushes me so I sit on the edge of my bed. Removes my socks, my pants, my underwear, tossing them into a pile of discarded clothes in a corner. She lifts my feet so I can lie down on the bed. Pulls the covers over me.

I lie on my side and she leaves the room. I hear her pad around the house, locking doors, turning out the lights, feeding the cat. She comes back into my dark room, removes all her clothes, and climbs in beside me.

She spoons me. The warmth of her body and the calmness of her breathing lulls me to sleep.

The Best

When I wake, I'm alone. I roll over onto my stomach, lying diagonally across the bed. I rest my head on Rhonda's pillow, pulling her aroma into my nose. It's a mix of her body odour, hair products, laundry detergent, and many other things that she comes in contact with through her day, all part the fragrance of Rhonda. For the most part her scent is something I notice subconsciously, but when I roll over and rest my head on her pillow, I wonder briefly if I have an odour, and if Rhonda knows it.

Of course, she does.

It's raining, a watery hiss coming from outside. But as I waken further, I notice popping and splattering sounds along with the hiss. And a distinctive smell coming from the kitchen. It's not raining; Rhonda is frying bacon. I know that because the only person in this house who actually cooks bacon is me. J and K are afraid of frying bacon.

The sweet, meaty smell of the bacon pulls me out of sleep and soon out of bed. I slip on a T-shirt and a pair of sweats and walk down the hallway into the kitchen.

Rhonda is standing by the stove—yes, frying bacon. And making toast. And eggs.

My two brothers sit at opposite ends of the table, J behind a book, K behind his iPad, ignoring each other but forced to come out from behind their respective reading materials to take bites out of their respective meals.

I stand next to Rhonda and put an arm around her. "You're the best."

She hands me a plate with bacon, toast, and two over-easy eggs. "I know."

Talk

After he finishes his meal, K puts down his tablet. "Will you need a lawyer? I know several who can offer a reduced fee."

I shake my head. "I haven't been charged with anything so I don't think a lawyer is necessary."

"Did the police tell you that? That you are not a suspect?"

"They said I was a person of interest."

"Which means you're a suspect."

"Technically, yes. But one of the constables told me there was nothing to worry about."

"That's what they want you to think. I would recommend getting a lawyer. I'll talk to some friends today."

"Man, you don't always have to take over and think you're saving the day, you know," J says. "Sometimes we can handle problems ourselves."

"Yes, everything's hunky dory, isn't it? M is a suspect in a murder—"

"I'm not really a suspect," I cut in.

"M's not really a suspect," J repeats. He sits up high in his chair, as if poised to attack. K is sitting the same way. He looks at both of us and shakes his head.

"K is right," Rhonda says. Their postures relax at the sound of her voice. Because Rhonda has no family baggage, she is seen as neutral. "Regardless of what the constable told you, you are a suspect in a murder investigation. I think it's wise to get some outside help."

A moment's pause. K stands up, grabs his tablet and his phone.

"I'll make some calls."

Suspended

Rhonda takes her uniform from my closet and gets dressed. "Officially, you're suspended for a week."

"A week. That's not fair. I'm not really a suspect and I did nothing wrong."

Rhonda buttons her shirt and slowly turns around. "Seriously? That's your defence?"

The angry look on her face makes me step back to sit on the bed.

"Your being a suspect has nothing do to this."

"Then why?"

"You want a list? Let's start with accepting a gift from a citizen you were investigating."

"It was only tea and cookies."

"Still against the guidelines. Let's not forget the nap and the speeding."

"I can explain those."

"And you'll be able to. But not now."

"So, I'm being punished."

"Prior to this, would you have taken anything, even a drink of water, from a citizen you were investigating? Let alone fallen asleep on his couch?"

I can do nothing but shake my head. She steps forward and touches my cheek.

"You also need a break to get your shit together before you can go back to work. So do that."

Empty House

Rhonda and K have work. J is at school. The empty house feels strange. There are odd noises all over the place. Each one seemingly new and strange but once I search out its source, I discover that these are normal noises. Like the dripping in the back of the fridge, the hum of the water heater, the sound of the wood frame of the house expanding in the heat.

Being alone at home during the day is disconcerting. I take a walk. The weather is also odd. The wind is sporadic, blowing the clouds about. The sun goes in and out, so at one moment it's almost too hot, but then in the next it's almost too cool.

My walk doesn't last long.

Back at home, I light some sage, let the smoke blow over me. I'm too jittery for the smudge to work. I try to watch TV but then remember we cut the cable. Our streaming services offer me nothing. For half an hour I watch a documentary about a classic rock star but that gets old very quickly.

J has games in the basement, but I could never get into the type he plays. For a brief moment, I think about cleaning the house, but it's already clean.

I make myself lunch; it's not even eleven, but I'm bored. I get a little more elaborate than I should and make a lasagna. After that, I make two batches of cookies, eat a few, then pass another half-hour cleaning the mess I made in the kitchen.

The cookies taste good but I'm lost. And only one day of suspension barely over. I have four more to go. I'm in trouble.

Parallel Parking

The next day I have an appointment with a lawyer. K drives me because he knows the lawyer.

"Where did you find a lawyer who would meet with me so quickly?"

"He's a contact from the party," he says, as he searches for a parking spot downtown. "I made a few calls about your situation and someone set this up."

"Wouldn't my situation hurt your position in the party?"

"Don't be ridiculous," K says, laughing. He hasn't laughed for a while so it's nice to hear, even though it is at my expense.

"I didn't get into the details, I just told them a family member was having some kind of legal trouble with the police and that was that. They gave me the name of lawyer in the party, I contacted him and filled him in with some details." He spots an open parking spot. "Ah, here we go."

K parallel parks like an expert. "I'll admit they responded quickly, but apparently this kind of situation happens more than we think."

"What? Someone the party knows becomes a murder suspect on a regular basis?"

"Don't be silly." K's parking is almost perfect but he still moves the car back and forth to fit even better.

"I'm talking about legal problems, although your situation is a little more serious than most, I'm sure." K's parking is proper now and he starts to adjust his tie in the mirror.

"I really appreciate your help, K, but I'm worried about the cost," I say. None of us in the family makes a lot of money. Enough, but to pay for a lawyer? I'm not so sure.

"He's a contact from the party," K says. "And because of that, he's waiving his fee."

I open my mouth, but K holds up a hand. "Don't ask. Just let it go."

The Lawyer

The lawyer is a lot younger than I expect, probably only five or so years older than J. But his office is well appointed with oak furniture and a corner window looking out over the river valley. Based on these signals, I assume he's good at what he does, despite his youthful appearance.

I'm introduced but quickly forget his name as I look out the window.

I let K do all the talking, explaining the situation as best as he can. Surprisingly, he doesn't sound like he's disappointed in me. He phrases the story like I'm some kind of victim caught up in circumstances beyond my control.

The lawyer nods thoughtfully and even though he already knows the situation does not interrupt K once during his explanation. He only speaks when K is finished.

"The situation is a bit apprehensive, I'll admit that. But based on what you've just told me and what I've gleaned from the Crown's office, M is officially a suspect, but it's more along the lines of a person of interest. A witness. A suspicious witness. There are concerns, but based on my conversation with the Crown, so far there is nothing to be too worried about."

"You've talked to the Crown already?" K asks, eyes wide.

"Of course, of course," says the lawyer, waving his hand. "And there may be questions again, more DNA samples, but it's just procedure. I'll be there for both of those events."

"That's wonderful," K says.

"For all those lists and new members you've brought to the party, it's the least I can do," the lawyer says with a bright smile.

K offers his thanks yet I can't help but notice the quick look he sends my way. And how his face briefly turns red when he does so.

The Lists

On the third day of my suspension I have something to do. I tell everyone that I'm going to undertake a serious cleaning of the house but that's just a ruse. K and J are fastidious people; they are always cleaning up after themselves.

So while I clean, I also search. K wouldn't be dumb enough to leave important papers lying around, or just tucked into his desk. But he's also not as imaginative as he thinks he is. And I find the box tucked into the storeroom. On the outside it's marked TAXES, and it's true, there are some tax forms, etc. in the front of the box.

But at the back of the box, I find what I'm looking for: several lists. The first group is a list of the names, addresses, and phone numbers of members of various community groups that K's work has brought him into contact with.

The other is a list of new members of the political party that my brother belongs to. Every name from a community list is on the new member list.

The final list is the most damning. Every new member has checked the box stating they will allow their individual vote to be decided by a proxy. The handwriting on the membership card is identical. He's not named as the proxy—that would be stupid. There are several different names shown. But it's all K's handwriting.

I put the lists back into the box as I found them, and pack the box away. And then, as promised, I finish cleaning the house.

No Caller ID

The next morning, after making breakfast for my brothers and sending them off to work and school, I'm at a loss about what to do. The house is clean, there are enough cookies, and I don't wish to think about what my brother has done. Just before I turn on the television, I get a call on my cell.

"No Caller ID," it says. Everyone I know who calls me is entered into my contacts menu.

I put the phone back in my pocket and turn on the TV, choosing a sports documentary on the knuckle ball. I did not grow up with baseball but I find it intriguing. On the surface, it is a simple game but many miniscule details are involved. Not just about how to throw a ball or swing a bat, but the endless statistics, and the almost obsessive nature of how people collect them and use them.

My phone vibrates yet again. I pause the knuckleball documentary.

No Caller ID.

I wonder which unknown person would be calling me. The only two that come to mind are the police and my lawyer.

I sigh and answer the phone.

It is neither the police nor my lawyer.

"Is this the bylaw enforcement officer?" a familiar female voice asks.

I pause, trying to place the voice before I answer. "Who is calling, please?"

"It *is* you," the voice says excitedly. "I recognize your voice."

"Who is calling, please?"

"It's Yuri," she says. It takes me a second to remember who Yuri is and that the voice on the phone belongs to his wife.

"He's missing."

Please

"How did you get this number?"

"Did you not hear me? Yuri's missing."

"Call the police."

Pause. "I can't."

"Why not?"

When she says nothing in response, I continue. "The police can help you. I cannot."

"You must."

"Why? I'm only a bylaw enforcement officer. Call the police." I move to disconnect the call.

"Please," she says, her voice cracking, so pitiful yet honest that I cannot hang up.

"Call. The. Police."

"I can't."

"Why not?"

"Because . . ." Her voice breaks and she begins to cry. It takes twenty seconds for her to compose herself enough to answer.

"Because he's done this before."

"Done what before?"

"Gone missing."

"Then he'll come back."

"This time is different."

"How do you know?"

"Because I'm his wife," she shouts at me. Angry. Then crying again. "Please."

Indecision

I spend the next twenty minutes wracked with indecision. Obviously, the police can help Yuri's wife much more than I can. But since she said he went missing before and returned before, they would consider his behaviour a recurrence and would not help her.

But I have no authority to conduct such an investigation. Even going over to Yuri's house and talking with his wife could have implications for my already tenuous employment situation.

I am also a person of interest in a murder investigation relating to the murder of the Pyjama Man, Yuri's neighbour. And there was animosity between these neighbours, a fact I myself told the police in my statement.

Did Yuri's disappearance have anything to do with his neighbour's death? Did Yuri kill his neighbour? Did he put him under the Red Chesterfield? If Yuri didn't, then who did? What about the foot and the original Red Chesterfield? Is there any connection? If not, then who put the Red Chesterfield there? And why?

In the end, the Red Chesterfield is what gets me out of my indecision. And out the door.

To get answers. About the Red Chesterfield.

Empty Ditch

The first thing I check when the Uber drops me off at Yuri's cul de sac is the ditch where I found the Red Chesterfield. Where I found both Red Chesterfields.

The ditch is empty. I am both pleased and disappointed about this, a dichotomy of feelings I can't really explain. The last few days of my life have been the most unusual I have ever experienced, disconcerting and exciting at the same time. Another dichotomy I can't truly understand.

The yard sale is still in place, with the tarp and the junk. I walk through it and up to Yuri's door.

I look at the two wires of the doorbell and knock. I hear voices in the distance, whispers that sound worrying.

The door opens and I'm shocked to see Yuri standing in front of me. My mouth falls open and I stare at him.

"Well, what the fuck do you want?" he says.

When he speaks, I realize it is not Yuri but someone who looks like him. A brother? A cousin?

"Who is it?" I hear Yuri's wife ask from the living room.

The Lookalike looks me over. "Some Indian," he says with disdain.

A rustle of sounds and, seconds later, Yuri's wife is at the door, beaming at my presence. "You came."

"I did."

She grabs my hand and yanks me into house. She pulls me into a hug, squeezing the breath out of me.

The Lookalike steps back, but the look of distaste is still on his face.

Wail of Rage

"I'm so glad to see you," Yuri's wife says after she releases me from her hug.

I start to talk, something along the lines of "I'm not sure what I can do," when the Lookalike says something in an Eastern European language. I don't need to understand to know it's something derogatory, a comment about me.

The look of happiness on the face of Yuri's wife changes instantly to anger. She screams back at the Lookalike in the same language. He yells something in return.

She's frozen in shock at whatever he says, and I can tell that he instantly regrets saying what he said. But it's too late. Even though he makes apologetic sounds.

Yuri's wife explodes with rage. She pushes me aside, almost knocking me to the floor.

She swings several punches at the Lookalike. He puts his hand up to block them, but I can tell by the way he winces at each punch that they hurt.

He tries to placate her, apologizing over and over, but to no avail. She swings at him several times, is blocked repeatedly, and then stands in the middle of the living room. She screams and points at the front door.

"Wait, wait," the Lookalike says in English.

"I said, Get Out!" She screams and points to the door. "Get! Out!"

He looks at her, hoping for a reprieve, but even I can tell she won't change her mind.

He shakes his head and storms out, roughly shoving me aside as he goes by.

This time, I fall to the floor.

Yuri's wife screams once more. Not words in another language, but a wail of rage.

Short-Term Use

Violent outbreaks of emotions like I have just witnessed make me uncomfortable, and for a moment I'm pushed into the Blue Zone. And while I see Yuri's wife stomp out of the room and down the hallway, it doesn't register until a few seconds later. I'm left alone in the entryway of the house, unsure of what I'm supposed to do. I'm more used to K's passive-aggressive strategies or J's quiet non-communication. Rhonda's emotions are strong but steady. They can rise in intensity, but it's a slow rise, like a fire that burns so gradually that you're taken unaware of how warm you can become. And yet Rhonda's fire will never burn me—that much I know to be true.

My first desire at Yuri's house is to leave and go home. I don't know what Yuri's wife is doing. And if she wants me to stay.

Being in the Blue Zone doesn't help with my decision-making process.

I sit in the chair by the door, a button-tufted U-bench with dark wooden legs and a cushion the colour of oatmeal. The U-bench isn't as comfortable as the Red Chesterfield, but comfort is not the point of this chair. It's for decoration, one of the first pieces of furniture you see when you enter the house, and thus designed for short-term use.

If Yuri's wife comes out by the time the Blue Zone fades away, I'll stay. If not, I'll go home and forget all of this.

The Zones of Regulation

There are three Zones of Regulation that everyone deals with, whether they know they exist or not.

There's the Green Zone—the place for optimal learning and living. You aren't always happy in the Green Zone, but you are safe and fully aware of the world, responding to it from a good place in your brain.

Then there's the Blue Zone—sometimes confused with the Green Zone, because from the outside both can look the same. But for whatever reason, you shut down, either due to mood or for a desire to protect yourself from forces you don't think you can control. Many people live completely in the Blue Zone, thinking they are in the Green.

Finally, the Red Zone—this is a place of anger, fear, absurdity, and other intense emotions. It is obviously not a good place to live.

Cursed by Apollo

I'm not sure how long it takes for me to come out of the Blue Zone, but when I do Yuri's wife is standing in the middle of the living room, looking at me. I blush because I'm not sure how long she has been staring at me.

She smiles, light and soft, apologetic. "I'm sorry for the outburst, earlier. Yuri's brother can be so aggravating sometimes, so unlike Yuri."

That was his brother, I think, but she nods, and I realize that I spoke those words out loud.

"I expect it must have been disconcerting to see him answering the door," she says. "You probably thought it was Yuri."

I nod.

"They look so much alike—not twins, Yuri is the younger one, only a year younger than Boris, but in many ways a lot older. Boris can be such a child."

I nod, taking in the words, but something nags at me, something as yet unspoken. And although it has little to do with the Red Chesterfield, the finding of the foot, the neighbour's body, and the apparent disappearance of Yuri, I can't continue without getting past that gap.

"I'm sorry," I say, rubbing my eyes. "In my mind I keep calling you 'Yuri's wife,' but that's not proper. You know my name but I don't know yours."

She smiles. "Cassandra. My name is Cassandra."

"That's a beautiful name."

Her brown eyes sparkle. But then the smile turns sad.

"Beautiful and clever, say the legends, but insane," she says. "Cursed by Apollo when she refused to sleep with him. When she prophesied events to come, she was never believed."

Then I Am No Barbarian

I sputter some platitudes, telling her that my presence is proof of my belief in her statement.

A wave of her hand tells me that she knows that I'm not telling the complete truth and there is no need to continue.

"Please come in, if you wish. And sit. Or leave. I will not judge your choice." She stands in the middle of the room, her face blank.

Leaving isn't an option, whether or not I believe her story about Yuri being missing. I came here for my own reasons, so I enter the living room, sit on the sofa where I had my nap.

"Tea?" Cassandra asks. She remains in the spot in the middle of the living room but has turned 180 degrees to face me.

"Will you judge my choice in that?" I ask.

"Of course," she says with a laugh that defuses the tension in the room. "Anyone who refuses an offer of tea is a barbarian."

"Then I am no barbarian."

"I know. That is why I called you."

Jumbles

Cassandra serves the tea the same way Yuri did, in a small, delicate cup with a teaspoon of jam sitting on the saucer. I stir the jam through the tea while she goes back into the kitchen, returning with a plate of round cookies dusted with icing sugar. She holds out the plate for me and I take one, setting it down on the saucer next to my cup.

Cassandra sits on the opposite end of the sofa, a respectable distance away, crossing her legs. She takes one of the cookies and dips it into the tea, takes a bite.

I'm unsure of adding more sweetness to my tea, but follow her lead. There's a honey-nutty taste to the cookie, similar to a jumble cookie, almost a pastry but not quite, with a hint of nutmeg. Very tasty.

Since I'm not a detective of any sorts, only a suspended bylaw enforcement officer, I'm uncertain where to start. I focus on the tea. And the cookies.

"These are delicious."

"*Pyraniki*, basic Russian tea cookie. Simple to make. Before you go, I will give you the recipe, if you wish."

I nod. Drink my tea. Eat the rest of my cookie. Cassandra lifts the plate to offer me another. I demur but she insists by jerking the plate slightly. I acquiesce and take another one. Dip it in my tea and bite.

I can think of nothing to start a conversation about Yuri.

This Time Is Different

Mercifully, Cassandra begins. "You believe me when I say Yuri is missing?"

I have no idea what to believe. "You said he's gone missing before?"

She nods.

"But this time is different?"

She nods.

"What is different about this time?"

She drinks the rest of her tea, stands, goes to the samovar on the dining room table and pours herself a second cup.

"Yuri—." She starts but stops. Drinks more tea. Takes a deep breath. "Yuri is having an affair."

I blink quickly. Nothing comes to mind in response to that.

"With Boris's wife."

My blinking increases and I turn to the front door.

"Boris doesn't know," she says. "He works in a camp building towers for a new electrical line. When Yuri disappears before, he is with her."

"But not now?"

She shakes her head.

"How do you know for sure?"

"A wife knows."

"If you want me to believe you, you have to do better than that."

It takes her at least a minute.

"I called her. And she said he was not there."

"She could be lying."

She chuckles, but not as if she is laughing at a joke.

"My sister is a terrible liar."

Not What You Think

I'm so shocked that I'm only able to say "Your sister . . ." before my mind shuts down my vocal chords.

"It's not what you think," Cassandra says, waving her teacup at me.

I don't know what to think. First, Boris and Yuri, brothers, married to a pair of sisters. One of those brothers—Yuri—is having an affair with the other brother's—Boris's—wife. Who, again, happens to be the sister of Yuri's wife, Cassandra. And not only does Cassandra know about the affair, she has called her sister to ask if her missing husband is there. And because he is not, he must be missing.

What about Boris? Does he know? Was that why he was so angry? If so, does that mean he's involved somehow in Yuri's disappearance? Did he cause harm to his brother because he discovered Yuri was sleeping with his sister-in-law? His sister-in-law from both sides.

And what did he say to Cassandra to make her so angry, to make her explode in a scream of rage and throw him out of her house?

Questions, thoughts, and confusions whirl about in my mind so fast that they almost push me into the Blue Zone. Almost, but not quite.

Still, I have no words to offer Cassandra, just a look of incredulity.

She looks at me, again waving her teacup.

"It's not what you think," she says again, as if she's just read my thoughts.

Skirting the Edges

I pull myself back from the edge of the Blue Zone. "How do you know what I think?" It comes out a lot louder than I expect, almost a shout, which surprises Cassandra to her feet. But sometimes I need to jolt myself with a sudden movement or sound to get out of the Blue Zone.

Although I'm not sure if I'll fall into the Red Zone and completely lose it, which has been known to happen, or if I'll just get back into the Green Zone and skirt the edge.

"How could this affair of Yuri's with his brother's wife, who just happens to be your sister, not have anything to do with his disappearing? Perhaps Boris found out."

"Boris doesn't know."

"Maybe he does."

"He doesn't. I'm a quite sure of that."

"How can you be so sure?"

"Because if Boris knew that Yuri was having an affair with Helene, then Yuri would be dead: Boris would not hesitate to kill him."

I stare at her, my mouth wide open, my thought obvious from my expression.

Cassandra shakes her head at my look. "Boris doesn't know. Yuri isn't dead, he's just missing."

"How do you know?"

"Because he called me and told me to tell you that."

I Beg Your Pardon

"I beg your pardon?" I say. "He said you should tell me he is missing?"

Cassandra nods.

"Then he's not missing?"

"I don't know where he is, so technically he is missing."

"But not enough to go to the police?"

She nods. Lifts the plate of cookies to offer me another.

The movement is so incongruous with what we are talking about that I look at her as if she's insane. She shrugs and puts the plate down. There is a slight probability that she is insane. A spark flashes inside of me and starts to grow into a burning flame. It's the urge to flee and forget everything in this cul de sac. But I push it down, still skirting the edge of the zones but so far on the right side of green.

"Why me?" I ask. It's a question directed at Cassandra, but also at the universe in general—a response to all the events of the past several days.

"Yuri said you could be trusted."

"Yuri and I barely know each other. And I am the bylaw officer who keeps bothering and warning him about this yard sale."

"But you fell asleep on his couch. Yuri said that showed a lot of trust on your part."

"I was tired."

"Tired or not, if there were no sense of trust about Yuri and this house, you would not have fallen asleep."

"That's just silly."

She shrugs: "That's Yuri."

I Am Not a Sexual Being

I put down my teacup and saucer and run my hands over my face. It's taking all my strength to stay centred. "And what does Yuri want me to do?"

"He didn't say. He just said to call you and tell you he was missing. 'Play it up,' he said. 'If you act like a damsel in distress, the bylaw officer will come.'" She gives me a shrug.

I look at her, wondering if I'm always so easy to read.

She nods.

"So I'm just supposed to take it from you and go searching for Yuri. A man who may or may not be missing."

She nods again.

"This is insane."

Another nod. "That's Yuri."

"Why do you stay married to him?" I ask after a pause.

"You wouldn't understand."

"He sleeps with your sister."

"She's better equipped to deal with that side of our relationship."

"I do not understand this."

"I am not a sexual being—"

"I don't mean that," I shout, cutting her off. "I'm talking about all of this. It's completely insane."

She opens her mouth to speak and I leap to my feet and point at her. "And don't say 'That's Yuri.' That means nothing to me because I don't know Yuri."

"Then maybe you should."

Recipe

I throw my hands up in frustration. "This is just stupid," I say, making my way to the door. "If you hear from Yuri, tell him I'm going home and if he wants to stay missing, he can. I wish to have nothing to do with this anymore."

Cassandra stands as if she's saying goodbye after a normal visit. "Thank you for coming."

The situation remains absurd, but manners and protocol force me to speak. "Thank you for the tea. And the cookies."

She leaps to her feet as if she's forgotten something. "Yes, the recipe. You asked for the recipe for the cookies and I promised it." She moves through the dining room into the kitchen.

"That is not necessary," I say, but she ignores me. I hear rustling in the kitchen, the opening of a drawer or two, the snapping of paper. I know I should walk out of this house, never to return, but again, manners long ingrained force me to remain and wait.

After a few minutes, she comes into the entryway, waving a piece of paper. She hands it to me. I take it and she places both her hands over mine. "Thank you for coming."

"My pleasure," I say, but that's only manners and protocol talking.

She looks at her two hands over mine, then glances up and smiles at me. She releases me.

I nod, deeper than I expect, almost like the nods so carefully demonstrated in a Jane Austen movie.

I turn and leave the house, stuffing the recipe into my coat pocket, vowing never to return.

Boris

I walk to the road, repressing an urge to run. I fumble for my phone so I can call an Uber and get a ride. I open the app, but a large pickup pulls alongside of me, facing the other way, so the driver's door is next to me; the windows are tinted and I'm unable to see who is driving.

Then the window slides down and Yuri's brother Boris stares at me. "Get in," he says. He does not look happy.

I try to call 911 on my phone, but he senses the movement and furrows his brow. "Get in," he says again, his voice colder this time.

My muscles tighten with fear. I shake my head, a slow twist to the right and then the left.

He blinks at me. Then he pulls a pistol up from behind the door and holds it out, not quite pointing it at me, but not quite *not* pointing it at me.

"Get in," he says again in his icy voice.

My muscles tighten further. And then they loosen and explode into life as I run. Away.

Flashback #3

I was at the outer edge of a fence, near where the garbage cans are placed so the waste management contractors can pick them up. All around were plants, Canada Thistle and dandelion, the white puffs ready to burst.

The dandelion was fine—it's not a noxious weed. But the Canada Thistle was. Not a danger to the waste management contractors, because of their clothing, but Canada Thistle has an extensive root system. These plants were concentrated, their roots probably spread along the side of the fence and into the neighbour's yard.

I was writing a warning note when the homeowner showed up, carrying a hockey stick. "What the fuck are you doing?" he asked.

"We had a report of Canada Thistle."

He waved the hockey stick in my face. "You better leave."

"Are you threatening me?"

He looked at the stick and waved it again. "You better leave."

I stepped out of reach of his stick and held up my phone. "I'm dialling 911 if you don't drop the hockey stick. Uttering threats is an offence under the Criminal Code, especially when such threats are made to a peace officer.

"Shit, they're just weeds, no need to make a federal case out of it."

"Yes, they are just weeds. No need to go to prison threatening a peace officer because of weeds."

He dropped the hockey stick and backed away. At the corner, he rushed back into his yard, into his house.

I put the warning about his weeds in his mailbox.

Flashback #4

The homeowner stepped out of his front door barefoot, holding a hunting rifle in one hand. He stood at the top of his steps and pointed it at me.

"Get off my lawn."

Technically, I was not on his lawn. I was on the walkway from the main sidewalk and hadn't yet reached the bottom of his steps. But I wasn't going to argue the semantics with him. I dropped my bylaw ticket book and held up my hands, palms out. I could feel my body tighten with fear.

He smiled at that and raised the rifle a bit higher.

I stared at the barrel.

"Get off—"

I dashed away to the right, running along the front of his house, close to the wall. It took me only six steps and I was at the corner of the house. I raced around that and ran along that side of the house.

I heard him shout, "Hey!" but I kept running through his side lawn, then took a left turn to run along the back of the house. I jumped over bits of broken wood and debris near the back door and headed to the other side, where I knew a rundown gate led into the alleyway. This was not my first visit. I was quite familiar with the layout of the yard.

When I got to the alley, I turned right and ran north, away from the house. I didn't know where the homeowner was, but I didn't care. There was no way he could have chased me through his dangerous backyard barefooted.

As I ran, I called 911 on my phone, identified myself as a bylaw enforcement officer, and reported the threatening man with the gun.

The sound of sirens in the distance was almost instantaneous.

Run!

I run the length of Boris's truck, swerving directly behind and then along the road on the passenger side; if he decides to shoot, the angle of the shot will make it tough for him to hit me. But I don't think he will shoot. It's not the first time I've faced someone with a weapon. That's why I run.

He shouts, "Hey!" but by then I'm several metres from his truck and still running. Running towards the ditch at the edge of the cul de sac.

I hear the roar of his engine coming closer. He's reversing to drive after me.

But when I hit the ditch, I know he can't get me. His truck may be big, but the ditch is too deep. If he drives into it he will get stuck. Or, like me a few days back, flip the truck over on its side.

Across the ditch and then I'm on the shoulder of the road that it runs alongside. Traffic isn't that bad, but I have to run about ten metres before there's enough of a gap to sprint across the road. Horns blare and tires screech, but I do not slow. I make it across four lanes of traffic and cross the ditch on the other side. Into that neighbourhood, weaving between houses for several blocks until I find a small green space with trees and bushes.

I push through the branches, ignore the scratches on my arms and face, and find a secluded spot. I collapse on the ground, knowing it will take a long time for my breathing to slow and the shaking to stop.

Escape

I wait in my green space hidey-hole until it gets dark. Then I wait a bit longer. It's the cold that gets me out of there.

I think about calling someone for help, maybe K or Rhonda, but I don't want to put them in danger. Even though Boris didn't look like he would use his gun, I can't be too careful.

I step out of the trees and bushes, trying to look like someone who's searching for something. A lot of people own dogs these days, and there's always somebody walking a dog. So I have to be careful.

There's nobody.

I brush myself off and walk west, away from Yuri's house. Then I walk about thirty blocks west and another twenty-five or so blocks south, through various neighbourhoods I have seen in the course of my work. I come out onto a semi-major arterial road, which I know has some bus routes. I stand at a stop for about twenty minutes before a bus comes.

I take that bus to a transit centre farther west and transfer to another one heading downtown. I get off near the library and walk three blocks to the east, where I know I can get a bus heading north. I transfer to another bus that drops me off about three neighbourhoods from my house and I walk home.

The whole time, I'm looking over my shoulder, wondering when Boris will show up with his gun.

No One Home

There's no one home when I arrive, which is strange, considering how late it is.

But at least there's no one to see the dirt on my clothes and the scratches on my face and arms.

These scratches sting when I shower, but I don't stay under the water as long as I did after I found the foot.

Even after my shower, no one's home. I grab a quick bite, half a bagel with cream cheese, but although I haven't eaten since Cassandra's tea and cookies my stomach can only handle so much.

I climb into bed, thinking it will take me a long time to get to sleep, but I'm so exhausted I'm out within seconds.

Dream

I dream . . . of nothing. Again.

No Coffee

J shakes me awake.

"Wake up, M, wake up!"

I sit up quickly, ready to run from Boris and his gun again, then calm down when I see J. His face is full of worry. "Where were you all day yesterday? You were home when I left but then you were gone when I came back?"

"Where was I? Where were you? When I came home there was nobody here."

"I went over to Sid's house?"

"You stayed there all night?"

J shakes his head but blushes, revealing the truth.

"You know how K feels about sleeping over."

"Come on, I'm an adult. What big deal is it if I stay at my girlfriend's house? You do it all the time."

I shrug because I don't care if J stays out late with his girlfriend or otherwise. As he said, he's an adult.

"Anyway, K won't find out because I don't think he's been home all night."

"Maybe he left early. He does that sometimes."

"There's no coffee left in the machine," he says, with a shake of his head.

I look at my brother with surprise. "No coffee?"

"No coffee."

"Then where could he be?"

After a moment, J looks at me more closely.

"Hey, what happened to your face?"

Coffee

At the dining room table J and I drink coffee, eat some of the bagels he toasts for us.

"I tried calling him, but all I got was voicemail," he says. "Several times, only voicemail."

"Maybe I should call him, 'cause ..." I don't finish my sentence because I don't want to insult my brother.

"He might be blocking me," J says, without feeling any insult. He looks at me and shrugs. "Happens all the time. I block him too."

I call my older brother. Voicemail. "Hey K. It's me. M. Just checking up on you. Give me a call when you get this."

I set my phone down, and the instant I do it vibrates. Call display shows a blocked call.

J sees it too. "Answer it. Could be him," he says.

Could be Boris. Or Cassandra. Or Yuri.

"You going to answer it?" J asks.

After a moment, I do.

"Hello."

"This is Detective Mason of the police service. I'm calling about the body found under the red couch?"

"Yes, the Red Chesterfield?"

"Yes. The chesterfield." A pause. "I'm informing you that we are only going to consider you a witness in the case, rather than a suspect."

"Has there been a development about the Red Chesterfield?"

"All I can say is that you are now just a witness. You may be asked to testify about the events you witnessed related to the case, but that is all. You will be informed if this is so. Have a good day."

The call is disconnected and I'm left staring at the phone.

"Was that him? Was it?"

Lawyer Calls

I don't have time to answer J because my phone starts to ring again. Another blocked number.

"Hello?"

"Yes, this is Jon Smythe from Neumann Associates."

"Excuse me? Who?"

"Your lawyer. The one representing you in your case regarding the body found in the red couch."

"You mean the Red Chesterfield."

"Yes, the red chesterfield. I've been advised by the Crown that you are no longer a suspect in the case."

"I've heard that from the police. They just called me."

"They are efficient. Be that as it may, our dealings with you are complete. Please be advised that we will be severing any contact with you after this moment. And due to the situation with your brother, we'd ask you not to contact us again."

"What situation with my brother?"

"You are unaware of what occurred last night?"

"What happened last night?"

A pause. "I am not at liberty to say. I would talk to your brother."

"My brother is not here."

"It would be best to hear the news from him. I'm sorry I'm unable to continue with this call. Have a good day."

Our Brother Is an Idiot

"Who was that?" J asks.

"That was my lawyer, you know, the one K got me. I guess I'm not a murder suspect anymore."

"Hey, that's great news," J says, offering a fist bump. I don't leave him hanging.

"Still . . ." I start, then pause.

"What? Is there something else?"

"Yeah but it's odd, the lawyer kept mentioning the situation with K last night."

"With K? What situation?"

"He didn't say. Did K have a meeting or event last night?"

"Some meeting, I think," J says after a moment. "Some nomination prelim for his party."

My mind explodes in realization. I remember finding those membership forms in the storeroom. "Shit," I say, jumping to my feet. I rush down to the storeroom, J right behind me.

I throw open the box marked TAXES and rummage through the papers. "Where are they? Where are they? K, I hope you weren't being an idiot."

"What are you talking about?" J says, trying to see what I'm doing. "What are you looking for? Why is our brother an idiot?"

The papers are still there. But the Chromebook is gone. I step away and sit down on the floor. A deep sigh.

"What?" J says, kicking me gently to get my attention. "What?"

I look up at him. "Our brother is an idiot."

I Am an Idiot

J and I return to the table. I explain the membership papers I found in K's box, how I suspected him of forging party memberships to ensure his candidate would be selected for the nomination.

Halfway through my explanation, J shakes his head. "Our brother is an idiot."

"That's what I'm saying. There's more."

"Oh God," he says. "How can it get any worse? Is he doing drugs?"

I smile, thinking how silly it looks, not just K doing drugs, but J, the little brother we always try to protect, asking if his older brother is doing them.

"It's about me," I say.

"It's not your fault you found that foot," J says, reaching a hand out to touch mine. "And you're not a suspect anymore."

"There's more."

"Like a leg? Or an arm?"

I shake my head, take a breath, and tell him the whole story, everything that happened after my finding the foot, including my hours-long trek through the city last night in order to evade Boris and his gun.

When I finish, J just stares at me, disappointment in his eyes. He shakes his head, picks up his tea and stands up. "Fuck you two. You're always on my case about doing the right thing and here you are, both of you, fucking up left and right."

He walks away from the table, heading towards the front door.

"J," I call out to him.

"You don't get to say anything about how I live my life."

"But what about K?"

"Especially him." He slams the door behind him.

Fire

I don't go after J because I have no time. I go into the basement, into the storeroom, and pull out the box marked TAXES. I carry it into J's area and set it down by the fireplace.

There are several large pieces of wood but no bits of kindling. I grab one log, take it into the laundry room. On the dryer there's a hatchet we use to chop large pieces of wood into smaller ones.

That done, I carry the pieces and stack them into a log cabin shape in the fireplace. Then back into the laundry to get some dryer lint. I scatter the dryer lint into the spaces of the log cabin and spark them with the lighter that sits on the mantelpiece.

It takes several minutes for the wood to catch completely, and then I gingerly place a couple of bigger logs on top. It takes more time for those to catch and for the fire to grow large enough.

I throw the bits of paper in—not in one bunch, because that will just smother the fire, but in small batches. I wait for each batch to burn before I put another on the fire.

Two hours later, my job is complete.

The Whole Story

I haven't told J the whole story. There's a part of my and K's life that he knows nothing about. He wouldn't understand. Sometimes I barely understand it myself.

But it's there and it's part of our lives. And remembering it gives me a clue as to where K could be.

I take a shower, dress in some clean clothes, and head out the door.

The Uber driver picks me up and we make simple small talk about the weather as he drives me to my destination.

Upon arrival, I get out and wait for a moment at the edge of the sidewalk. I rate my driver very well to take up some time. Then I take a deep breath and walk up the sidewalk.

Normally, I would knock on the door and enter on my own. I do have a key. This time I ring the doorbell and wait.

Nothing happens, so I ring again. I hear footsteps inside the house and see a shadow through the window. The door opens and she stands there, looking at me.

Rhonda.

She's wearing a bathrobe over her pyjamas.

"Is he here?" I ask.

A pause. A deep sigh. A nod.

She pulls the door open wider and steps aside to let me in.

"He's in the bedroom."

I move past her to go talk to my brother.

Rhonda's Bedroom

K, shirtless, is sitting up in Rhonda's bed, in a spot I sometimes occupy, drinking a cup of tea. A piece of toast with peanut butter and jam, something he would never eat at home, sits on a plate next to him.

He sees me and responds the same way Rhonda did. A pause. A deep sigh. "You found me."

I nod but don't sit on the bed because, at the moment, I don't belong. "We were worried."

"We?"

"Me and J. You didn't come home last night ... And we heard about the nominations."

He blinked. "Who told you?"

"The lawyer."

A brief look of fear comes over his face. "Which one?"

"The one you hired for me. Because of the foot."

"Bastard," K says, setting down his teacup.

Some tea sloshes onto the floor and I feel bad for Rhonda: she hates spills.

"He wasn't specific, he only intimated there was a problem. I figured out the rest myself."

"You were spying on me."

"You were careless."

"I was ..." my brother starts to say. He closes his eyes, and the look of indignation fades from his face. When his eyes open again, he looks at me, pleading.

"I need your help."

"Of course. We're family. That's what we do."

Rhonda's Bed

I sit on the bed next to K, place a hand on his shoulder. "Is there any way that they can connect the situation to you?"

"Of course, they know it was me. That's why I'm out."

"I meant legally."

He pauses, then shakes his head. "I did all of the registering away from the house, using public Wi-Fi."

"Not with your own—"

"I'm not an idiot. I bought a Chromebook specifically for the project. Didn't use it for anything else. No surfing, no Facebooking, so it can't be traced to me."

"Where is that Chromebook?"

"Long gone. In pieces."

"Anything else?"

He sighs. "Only the membership lists, which I stupidly left in the house."

"You don't have to worry about that."

"I do. Someone mentioned asking the police to investigate, which means they may search the house and find them. If they do, I'm sunk."

I squeeze his shoulder. "No. They won't."

"But—" He pauses and gives me the look that he always gives me when he realizes again that I'm the smarter sibling. "You found them."

I nod. "In the fireplace."

The tension he was holding fades into a long, deep sigh. "Thank you."

"You're welcome."

I stand and move to leave the room. "Finish your toast and tea, then rest, okay?"

K nods.

Rhonda's Hallway

Rhonda stands in her hallway by the front door, flipping through fliers. I'm quite sure she hasn't read a single one in the time I was with K.

"He okay?" she asks, looking up.

"He'll be fine. You should go to him."

She touches me lightly on the arm. "Are you sure?"

"Yes. He needs you now."

"What about you?"

"I'm fine. And it's not my turn."

She removes her hand and steps aside to let me pass and leave the house.

I open the door, turn, and smile at her.

"I'll call you later," she says.

"Actually, I'll see you Monday." A pause. "At work."

She blinks several times, wondering how to respond to that. Then she nods, accepting my proposition. "Yes, that would make sense," she says. "You are ready to come back."

"So, Monday?"

She nods, looks back quickly, then steps up to me, kissing me on the side of the cheek, her hand resting on my side as if we are about to dance.

"Thank you. For helping him. And me."

I touch her hand on my side, hold it there for several seconds, then pull back and leave the house.

Ashes

I walk to the nearby mall before calling an Uber. I'm dropped off at the front of the house. I go inside. And clean.

Dust the surfaces, sweep the hardwood, vacuum the scattered bits of carpet, empty the dishwasher, fill it up again, wash the dishes not suitable for the dishwasher, clean the counter, the stove, sweep then mop the linoleum, move to the bathroom, clean the toilet, sink, and shower, including the tiles, sweep and mop that linoleum.

Muscles in my back, shoulders, arms, and legs start to ache, especially, because of my accident, my shoulder and neck. My hands are chafed and smell of cleaning liquid. I gather the recycling, tie up the blue bag, and toss it onto the front steps to be removed later.

I dig out the garbage bag under the sink, look at it for a moment, then head downstairs.

J is sitting on his couch playing his game.

"Did you find K?"

"I did. He's fine. He's at a friend's house."

"I didn't know he had friends."

"You'd be surprised."

"Did you clean up?" he asks, glancing over his shoulder.

"I did."

"Well, don't start down here because you'll be interrupting me."

"I'm only cleaning one thing." I head to the fireplace and sweep the ashes into the garbage bag.

"You don't have to do that," J says, not moving from his spot. "I can do it later."

"It's okay, I got it."

With all the ashes in the bag, I tie it and head upstairs without saying anything. We can talk later, if we talk about it at all.

I grab the recycling on my way out, dump the garbage bag into the bin, set the blue bag on the ground next to it.

Monday

I get up, dress for work, head out the door. I take the bus because my work truck is at the office lot. The bus is full, no place to sit, so I stand the whole way, rocking back and forth as the bus stops and starts along its route. There a couple of people from my work on the bus with me, but they ignore me, trying hard not to make eye contact.

It's the same once I get to the office. The space goes quiet as soon as I walk in. The only response I get to my "Good mornings" is people turning and walking away. Or pretending I don't exist. I don't care. I go to my office, get my assignments for the day, pack up my work gear, grab my keys, and start out on my shift.

I walk past Rhonda's office; she's sitting behind her desk with her head in a pile of paperwork.

"Hey, Rhonda."

She looks up, pen paused over the sheet of paper. She blinks and then smiles, not showing her teeth, but her eyes are welcoming nonetheless.

"Good day so far?"

"Seen better."

I nod and we look at each other for several seconds.

She blinks again. "Get to work," she says, half-serious. Back to her paperwork.

I salute. "Yes boss."

Graffiti

There's a building in the north end with graffiti on one wall.

I stare at the writing on the wall, turning my head sideways in an attempt to decipher the words. "Jac-Ca . . . acth," I say as I slowly mouth the words.

"I think the J is supposed to be a Q and the C a stylized Y or something," says the manager of the real estate office, a fit guy who looks like that hotel captain character from the commercials. "Maybe it's a V, I don't know."

"So it's Qacvyet?

"Makes no sense."

I start writing in my book.

The real estate manager sees me and frowns. "So, what happens now? When does the city come and clean this up?"

"This is private property. This isn't the city's responsibility."

"Then whose is it?" he asks, his face starting to turn red and his language clipped.

"Depends on who owns the building?"

"I own the building."

"Then it's your responsibility to clean it up."

"But I'm the one who called it in, using the city graffiti hotline."

"Thank you for exercising your civic duty." I rip the paper from my pad and hold it out to him.

"What's this?

"It's a notice, saying you have thirty days to clean up the graffiti or the city will come and do it for you and send you a bill."

He stares at me like I've just told him the Tooth Fairy isn't real.

I still hold the paper out.

"Jesus fuck," he says, snatching the paper from my hand. He reads it. "Jesus fuck," he says again before he balls up the paper and tosses it at me. He storms back into his office.

I pick up the ball of paper, unroll it, and then stick it in the mailbox.

Supper

K is back when I come home at the end of the day. He's standing in the kitchen, a sure sign he's contrite and wishes to make amends for his behaviour. The smell of roast chicken hangs in the air.

He greets me with a wave over his shoulder as he pours the rice into the colander. "You want a beer? There's cold ones in the fridge."

I don't usually drink on a work night but a beer does sound good. I get one, a local craft lager and snap it open. I take a sip and it feels cool and refreshing. I look at K cooking, at the table set. I know his contrition, though honest, won't last. But I say nothing. Best to just accept it.

"I'm going to change," I say, and go into my room with my beer. I set it on the end table, on an old sock so I don't leave a ring, and change out of my uniform. I think about washing it for tomorrow, but put aside that thought. Sometimes it's okay to let things go. Although I hang it all in the closet, rather than toss it on the floor like J would.

And he is sitting at the dining room table. He, too, has a beer, so we silently toast to the fact of K's actions. Even though we both know it won't last.

K comes bearing the food, describing what he has made for us.

J and I both nod and make the right positive sounds, so K serves us, then sits down and eats.

"Thanks, K," I say, nudging J under the table with my foot.

"Uh yeah, thanks K, smells great."

And it is great. K is a great cook, but sometimes feels cooking is beneath him.

We compliment him after our first bites and all's well and good. We eat, silently, like we always do, but there is no animosity in the silence, no passive aggression. That may come later, but for now, it's a simple quiet. Which is good.

Dessert

At dessert, J speaks. "I hope you two are done with your games."

K looks up, angry, seems ready to speak.

J interrupts before he can start. "You, with your political machinations. That has to stop."

K's anger fades to shame and he quietly returns to eating his ice cream.

"And you," J says, turning to me. "You have to stop."

"I wasn't involved, I only helped to end it."

"I'm not talking about that. I'm talking about the other games. Yes, finding the foot and that body were terrible for you, but instead of dealing with them in a mature way, you acted like some kind of private detective, trying to solve the crime. That's not your job, that's the job of the police."

Like K, there is nothing for me to do but to sheepishly eat my dessert.

"You were a murder suspect. You almost lost your job. Someone threatened you with a gun," J reminds me. "You almost lost Rhonda, and losing Rhonda would destroy this family."

He stares at me, then looks at K, letting his words of chastisement settle in.

I am beginning to wonder if J knows. He really is the smart one in the family.

"We can't lose that. Family," he says, tone softening. "That's the most important part of life. We have to protect that."

Back to Normal

The frosty attitude from my co-workers starts to melt. A few people wish me good morning, and by the end of the week, it's all back to normal. The idea that I suffered some sort of minor post-traumatic stress due to my discovery of a dead body and a severed foot has softened the hard feelings my other actions may have caused. I was not completely myself, but I sought help during my time off and returned to normal.

I have been forgiven my trespasses and welcomed back into the fold. Bringing doughnuts and pastries a few days in a row also helps ease the tension.

After exchanging some pleasantries (and the doughnuts) in the coffee room, I grab my gear to head out for my shift. I pass Rhonda's office, and again she is head down in her paperwork.

"Hey, Rhonda," I say, standing in her doorway.

She sees me and smiles, this time open and bright. "The doughnuts are amazing. Thank you."

"You're welcome," I say, pausing for a moment. "I was just heading out on my shift and realized that today is Friday."

"Yes, tomorrow will be the weekend." She looks down at her work. "Thank God."

"You want to see a movie or something? I figure I owe you that."

"You owe me a lot more than that," she says. But there is no animosity in her voice, just playful humour.

"So a movie would be a good start."

"Popcorn included?"

"Peanut M&M's too."

"You. After my own heart."

"That's the plan. So later? Tonight?"

"Yes. Later. Tonight."

Yard Sale Redux

I park my truck in front of Yuri's yard sale, pull out my ticket book, and write. I walk to the door, ring the doorbell.

Moments later, Yuri answers.

"Hey, it's you," he says, smiling. He pulls the door open wider. "Come in, come in. Have some tea."

I want to go in. I want to ask where he was, if he is okay. But my brother J is correct: my job is not to solve missing person cases. Or solve murders. Those are jobs for the police. I have sworn an oath to do another job.

"You are in continual violation of Part 6, Sections 2a, 2a.1, and 2a.2 of the Community Standards Bylaw and thus subject to a fine," I say, holding out the ticket. "If you continue to violate such sections, and if you do not clean up your yard according to community standards, the city will be forced to do so and you will be responsible for the cost of the cleanup. Any further violations after said cleanup will result in more fines, up to $10,000 per violation."

Yuri's smile disappears. "What the fuck is—"

"Do you understand?" I continue to hold out the ticket. A pause. "Do you understand?"

After a moment, Yuri spits on the ground near my feet.

"Fuck! You!"

Slams the door.

I deposit the ticket and a brochure outlining the Community Standards Bylaw in the mailbox.

I head back to my truck, my duty complete.

Red Chesterfield Redux Part 2

Before I get into my truck, I can't help but look toward the ditch where I first saw the Red Chesterfield.

I freeze and almost faint in shock when I see another Red Chesterfield there. It must be an illusion. A hallucination. I close my eyes, hoping it will be gone when I open them again.

But it's not.

The same Davenport-style Red Chesterfield sitting in the ditch. The same incongruous placement.

I am compelled to walk over.

I climb into the ditch and circle the Red Chesterfield a number of times.

I can't help it.

I sit.

It is, again, a very comfortable piece of furniture. It's soft without being too pliable and firm without being too hard. I can easily imagine sitting on this for a long period of time to read a book. Or to watch TV. Or to have a nap.

I sit there, asking questions I asked myself a while ago. Who put the Red Chesterfield here? Whose foot did I find in the original Red Chesterfield? Who put Pyjama Man under the other Red Chesterfield? Was he murdered? Did Yuri do it? Boris?

The last time I tried to get answers to these questions, I almost lost my job, my girlfriend, and I had to run and hide from a man who pulled a gun on me.

I have a family to worry about, Rhonda included.

Then again, I have to do something. I can't just sit here and leave the Red Chesterfield.

A Nice Piece of Furniture

I pull my truck out of Yuri's cul de sac. I park on the road on the other side of the ditch, on the grass so I don't block traffic. I get out and climb into the ditch where the Red Chesterfield sits.

I grab one end of the Red Chesterfield and lift. It's a bit heavy, but nothing I can't handle. It takes me several minutes to drag it out of the ditch and up to my truck. I open the tailgate of the truck and lift one end of the Red Chesterfield to rest on the edge. Then I lift the other side and slide the Red Chesterfield in. Part of it sticks out from the box but I have plenty of rope and bungee cords to tie it down.

J and K, even Rhonda, will probably question me about this, maybe even make a bit of a fuss.

But then they'll see that it's such a nice piece of furniture.

Photo of the author by Shawna Lemay

WAYNE ARTHURSON is a writer of Cree and French Canadian descent. He is the author of five novels, including *Fall From Grace*, winner of the Alberta Reader's Choice Award, and *Traitors of Camp 113*, a finalist for the High Plains Book Award for Best Indigenous Novel.

BRAVE & BRILLIANT SERIES

SERIES EDITOR:
Aritha van Herk, Professor, English, University of Calgary
ISSN 2371-7238 (Print) ISSN 2371-7246 (Online)

Brave & Brilliant encompasses fiction, poetry, and everything in between and beyond. Bold and lively, each with its own strong and unique voice, Brave & Brilliant books entertain and engage readers with fresh and energetic approaches to storytelling and verse, in print or through innovative digital publication.